"Bring me flesh and bring me wine, bring me pine logs hither,
Thou and I shalt see him dine, when we bear them thither."
Page and monarch forth they went, forth they went together,
Through the rude winds wild lament and the bitter weather.

"Sire, the ni... ows colder;
Fails my ... nger."
"Mark my ... them boldly,
Thou shal... ood less coldly."

In his mas... y dinted.
Heat was ... nted.
Therefore ... rank possessing,
Ye who nor... lves find blessing.

For Fiona's baby
A.E.

Text copyright © 1991 by Jean Richardson
Illustrations copyright © 1991 by Alice Englander

Calligraphy by Miriam Stribley

First edition

**Library of Congress Cataloging-in-Publication
Data**

Richardson, Jean.
    Stephen's feast / Jean Richardson; illustrated
by Alice Englander. — 1st ed.
    p.   cm.
    Summary: Stephen, the youngest page at the
court of King Wenceslas, is asked to accompany
his monarch on a mission of good will to a poor
peasant.
    ISBN 0–316–74435–2
    1. Wenceslas, Duke of Bohemia, ca. 907–929
— Juvenile fiction.
    [1. Wenceslas, Duke of Bohemia, ca. 907–929
— Fiction. 2. Carols — Adaptations.]
I. Englander, Alice, i11. II. Title.
    PZ7.R39485St 1991
    [E] — dc20   91–6392

Published in Great Britain by
J. M. Dent & Sons Ltd. Publishers

10 9 8 7 6 5 4 3 2 1

Printed in Italy

Jean Richardson
STEPHEN'S FEAST

Illustrated by Alice Englander

Little, Brown and Company

Boston   Toronto   London

Stephen could hear impatient voices calling his name as he crouched in his hiding place. The others would never find him here, he thought proudly.

He would show them he was just as clever as they were — as the youngest and smallest page in the palace, he was always being teased.

"Where has the boy got to?" That was a voice Stephen feared. "Trust him to vanish just when he's needed. What am I to tell the king? We can't find his page because he's playing hide-and-seek?"

The king! Stephen's heart thudded at the news that the king wanted him.

So far, Stephen had seen the king only from a distance.

Why should he want him now? And today of all days, when it was Stephen's birthday and the feast of the saint after whom he was named. Having a birthday so close to Christmas meant only one set of presents, but this year Stephen didn't care. The feasting and celebrating that went on in the palace were far grander than any birthday party could be.

Anxiously Stephen slipped out of his hiding place and presented himself to the angry chamberlain.

"About time! Don't you know you must never keep the king waiting? Hair like a haystack, filthy as a cellar rat! Clean yourself up, boy."

King Wenceslas was sitting by the window, looking out across the square.

"Come over here, boy," he called, "and tell me what you see."

Stephen obeyed him, wondering what he was supposed to say. Surely the king knew only too well what lay outside his own palace.

It was getting dark, and at first all Stephen could see was a blanket of snow, deep and crisp and even because no one had ventured out.

"That's a man, isn't it?" the king said, pointing to a dark shape in the snow. "Do you know who it is?"

Stephen was too far away to see the man's face, but he knew who it was. The man was often in the square, and Stephen and the other boys were used to making fun of him. Only last week Stephen had thrown a snowball at him.

"I think" — he hesitated — "They say he's a poor man who lives on the other side of the forest, near Saint Agnes's fountain. He comes looking for things . . . firewood . . . and scraps from the kitchen."

The king looked thoughtful. "Does he indeed. Well, today I'm going to give him a surprise. And you're going to help me."

Why me? Stephen thought crossly as he got ready.
What a stupid idea — even if it was the king's — to
take food and drink and logs to some miserable peasant
who lived far away.

He pulled on his new fur boots — a present from his
mother — and thought longingly of the games he
would be missing, of the great fire of logs hissing in the
servants' hall, of the spit on which a whole ox was
roasting.

As he wrapped his cloak around him, the very thought of the snow making him shiver, he wondered whether he should take his new hunting knife. It was his proudest possession. With it in his belt he felt like a man. And who knew what dangerous animals there might be in the forest?

The cook had loaded a small sledge with food and drink, and Stephen pulled it behind him. He could still smell the wonderful aroma of the roast meat. The cook had promised to save him some, but Stephen longed to stay in the Great Hall with its warmth and music and laughter.

The king led the way, carrying a sack of logs on his shoulder. The snow came up to Stephen's knees in places. The icy wind brought tears to his eyes. It raised clouds of loose snow, and Stephen couldn't see where he was going. Suddenly he stumbled and fell. He called out in frozen fear when he realized the snow threatened to bury him.

"I want to go back," he sobbed. "I'm frightened. I can't go on anymore."

The king lifted him up, dusted off the snow, and rescued the sledge. The frosted fur of his hat and beard glittered in the moonlight. He might have been a great bear.

"Courage, my little page," he said, and his voice was gentle. "You'll find it easier if you follow in my footsteps. The wind's cold enough to freeze your blood, but you'll soon thaw out when we get there."

They set off again, and this time Stephen was careful to tread in the king's footprints. He was right, it was easier to walk on the trodden snow.

He would have liked to ask the king why he cared about the peasant, but he hadn't enough breath to shout above the winter's rage. It occurred to him that the peasant must have wanted food and firewood very badly to venture out on such a bitter night. At the thought of how surprised and pleased the man would be, Stephen began to feel warmer.

Suddenly something gleamed ahead of them, and as they drew nearer, they saw an extraordinary sight. Saint Agnes's fountain had been transformed into a fairy-tale statue of ice that shone more brightly than all the candles in the palace.

"It's magic," Stephen whispered.

As they came to the edge of the forest, they saw a humble cottage at the foot of the mountain. The king called a greeting. The man and his family came to the door and couldn't believe their eyes when they saw the two figures in the snow: the tall, powerful man with his load of logs and the small, slight boy with his sledge.

Once inside the cottage, the king coaxed the miserable fire in the hearth back to life. As Stephen unpacked the food and wine, the family slowly began to understand what was happening.

Even so, Stephen could tell they hadn't realized who their visitor was — he certainly wasn't behaving like a king.

Soon there was a roaring fire, and the woman laid the table while the two youngest children sat on the king's lap. The eldest boy, who was about Stephen's age, looked wonderingly at him and gazed enviously at his hunting knife.

What a feast they had! Neither the children nor their parents had ever dreamed of such a spread. There was venison and roast pork, a plump goose, freshly baked bread, jellies and tarts, and an enormous spicy fruit custard. Soon they were all talking and laughing like old friends. Afterward, when they all swore they couldn't eat another morsel, there was still enough left for a second feast the next day.

Stephen could have spent all night talking to the boy in front of the fire, but the king insisted they must go.

By the time they reached the edge of the forest, Stephen had made up his mind what to do.

Swiftly he stole back to the cottage, felt for his precious hunting knife — and left it where the boy would be sure to see it in the morning. He knew the boy would treasure it even more than he did.

He ran back to join
Wenceslas, guided now by
his own footprints. It was
even colder now, but
Stephen's heart was as
warm as the king's, as
together they made their
way back to the palace.

King Wenceslas

John Mason Neale (1818 1886)

Good King Wenceslas looked out, on the Feast of Stephen,
When the snow lay round about, deep and crisp and even.
Brightly shone the moon that night, though the frost was cruel,
When a poor man came in sight, gathering winter fuel.

"Hither, page, and stand by me, if thou knowst it, telling,
Yonder peasant, who is he, where and what his dwelling?"
"Sire, he lives a good league hence, underneath the mountain,
Right against the forest gate, by St Agnes' fountain."